Daisy May

Kelly Belly

Laura Belle

Jeanne Marie

For my parents,

jim and nancy koehn;

my husband, pierce flynn jr., phd.;

and my sister, laura skaife.

Words cannot express how grateful I am for your love and support.

Also for the real-life Lulabellez who continually inspire me:

madelon gerety: Merry Berry the Cupcake Fairy

ariane brittany: Skye Pie the Dragonfly

anne hillenbrand: Annabelle

erika tuttle: Jada Pop

Copyright © 2010 by Lindsey Renee Skaife-Flynn.
All rights reserved. No part of this publication may be reproduced in any form without written permission from the publisher.

Library of Congress Cataloging-in-Publication Data available.
ISBN 978-0-8118-7685-8

Lulabellez created and designed by Lindsey Renee.
Additional text by Lissa Rovetch.
Book design by Tracy Johnson.
Typeset in Le Havre and Henparty Sans.

Manufactured by Leo Paper Products, Heshan, China, in July 2010.

10 9 8 7 6 5 4 3 2 1

This product conforms to CPSIA 2008.

Chronicle Books LLC
680 Second Street
San Francisco, California 94107

www.chroniclekids.com

What Kind of fairy Is Merry Berry?

by lindsey renee ♥ illustrated by lindsey renee and susan reagan

chronicle books·san francisco

Merry Berry was usually the $happiest$ little Lulabelle in Lulaland.

But lately, she felt gloomy, because Lulaland was just so dull and dreary!

The sun was not so $shiny$. The flowers were not so $bright$.

Even Merry Berry's cupcakes weren't tasting very sweet.

Like every little Lulabelle, Merry Berry had dreamed of becoming

a real live fairy

for as long as she could remember.

"Ho hum," she sighed as she strolled one afternoon with her cat, Pom Pom.
"I wonder what's wrong with Lulaland.
If only I could figure out a way to earn my fairy wings, I'd wave my magic wand

—swish swoosh—

and fix it just like that!"

Merry Berry strolled past droopy daisies and a grumpy honeybee.

"Ho hum," she sighed again. But then . . .

something shiny . . . something happy . . . something very, very bright . . . .

was twinkling over the hill!

Merry Berry ran to see.

There were sparkles on the houses! There were sparkles on the trees! There were sparkles everywhere!

Just then, a bright blue fairy flew by.

"I'm Skye Pie the Dragonfly," the fairy giggled. "Welcome to my world!"

"I've never seen such a sparkly place!" Merry Berry beamed.
"And I never *ever* knew there were dragonfly fairies!"

"Oh yes—there are many kinds of fairies,"
Skye Pie sparkled as she spoke.
"Different fairies with different gifts to share,
each with our own way to show
that we care!"

"I make garlands, bouquets, and little stone towers,"
Skye Pie said.

"I love being an artist with flowers!

And the best part of all is when I make someone's day,
by secretly giving my treasures away!"

"**WOW!**" said Merry Berry.

"Does my neighborhood ever need you!
It's been so dull and dreary lately. The sun's not so shiny.
The flowers aren't very bright. Even my favorite cupcakes aren't tasting very sweet."

"Oh, you don't need me," said Skye Pie.
"Everything will sparkle when you share in your own way!
I know you'll find your special gift and all the joy it brings.

Discover what you **love**, and you will earn your fairy wings!"

That evening in her room,
Merry Berry thought and thought.

More than anything,
she wanted to bring

sparkles

of happiness to her neighborhood
like Skye Pie the Dragonfly
brought to hers.

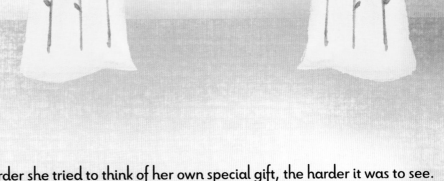

But the harder she tried to think of her own special gift, the harder it was to see.

Just then, she heard a *tippity-tap, tippity-tap* coming from the window.

When Merry Berry went to open the window, she could hardly believe her eyes!

"More fairies?" she said. "What an amazingly amazing day!"

"Guardian angel fairies to be precise," said one.

"My name is Jada Pop."

"And I'm Annabelle," said the other.
"We hear you've been looking for your special gift,
and we've come to lend a hand!"

"Everyone's gifts are different.
Everyone has something to share," said Annabelle.

"I teach my friends to dance.

That's my gift."

"And I teach my friends to $sing$," said Jada Pop.

"That's *my* gift!"

"You're so nice to come and help me," Merry Berry said.
"But what if I don't have any gift to share at all?"

"Don't say that!"
said Jada Pop.
"Just go to bed and
dream of the things
you love to do that could
brighten someone's day."

"That's what *fairies* do," said Annabelle.

"And that's how *you* can be a fairy, too!"

Well,
sleeping wasn't easy
after such a
magical
day.

Merry Berry
tossed and turned

until at last, she drifted off

and dreamed *sweet dreams* of all the things she loved.

And when
the morning came,
she had the answer . . .

Cupcakes!

"I love baking the very best cupcakes I can, for everyone to enjoy!" Merry Berry said.

Polka Dot cupcakes

Honey Bunny cupcakes

Rainy Day cupcakes

Giggle Pie cupcakes

Summertime
cupcakes

Kitty
Cat
cupcakes

Happy Daisy cupcakes

and So many more!

Merry Berry ran into the kitchen, and without another thought started baking the yummiest love-filled cupcakes imaginable!

And can you guess what happened when she gave those cupcakes to her friends?

Lulaland lit up with the happiest rainbow sparkles anyone had ever seen!

And can you guess what else?
A wonderful gift arrived, with a shimmering dress,
sparkly slippers, a pretty bracelet,
a magical cupcake wand,
and best of all . . .

. . . the most beautiful
fairy wings!

"Congratulations!" said the card,
"to Merry Berry the Cupcake Fairy."

What a perfectly perfect day!

That is how Merry Berry became

merry berry the cupcake fairy,

and that is how Lulaland became the happiest place around!

If you ever decide to visit, you will see for yourself,

that the sun is extra shiny, the flowers are extra bright,

and the cupcakes are extra, extra yummy!

Now
you
can find your
special gift.
What do you love to share?
Just take a look inside yourself.
The answer
is right there!